DRAGON'S SONG

Written by Jan Mike ■ Illustrated by Jean Pidgeon

MODERN CURRICULUM PRESS

PROJECT DIRECTOR: Susan Cornell Poskanzer
ART DIRECTOR: Lisa Olsson

MODERN CURRICULUM PRESS

299 Jefferson Road, Parsippany, NJ 07054
(800) 321-3106/www.mcschool.com

This edition is published simultaneously in Canada by Globe/Modern Curriculum Press, Toronto.

ISBN 0-8136-1180-6 (STY PK)   ISBN 0-8136-1181-4 (BB)   ISBN 0-8136-1182-2 (SB)

10 9 8   99

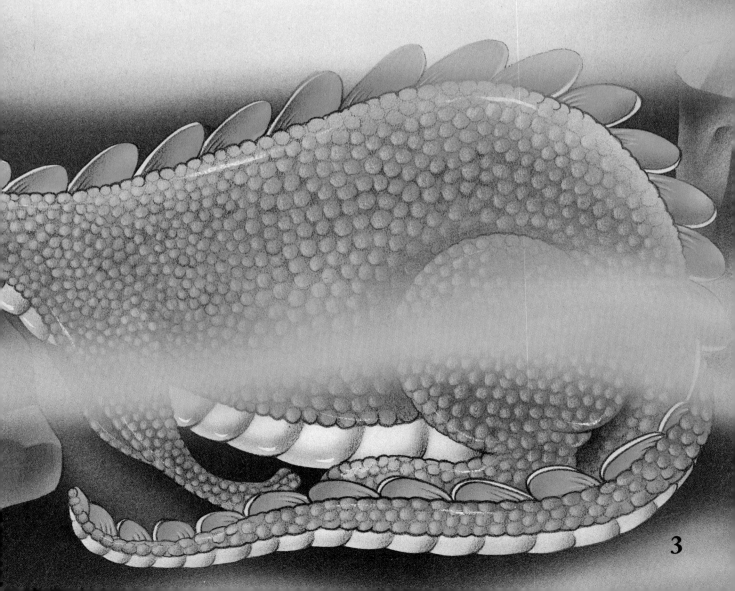

O nce upon a time, a great big dragon sat in his dark dreary cave on a bright sunny morning. He felt sad and lonely, and wondered what to do.

3

Outside Dragon's cave, a beautiful
lark perched on a nearby tree. She sang a
soft quiet song. She saw no one to sing to,
so Lark felt sad and lonely.

Dragon heard the bird singing.
"Ah ha!" said Dragon. "What I need is
a bird to sing in my cave. Happy songs
will make me feel cheerful."

5

Dragon peeked outside.
"Come into my cave, Lark," said
Dragon, "so I can hear you sing."
"No," said Lark looking into the cave.
"Surely, I could not sing in such a place."

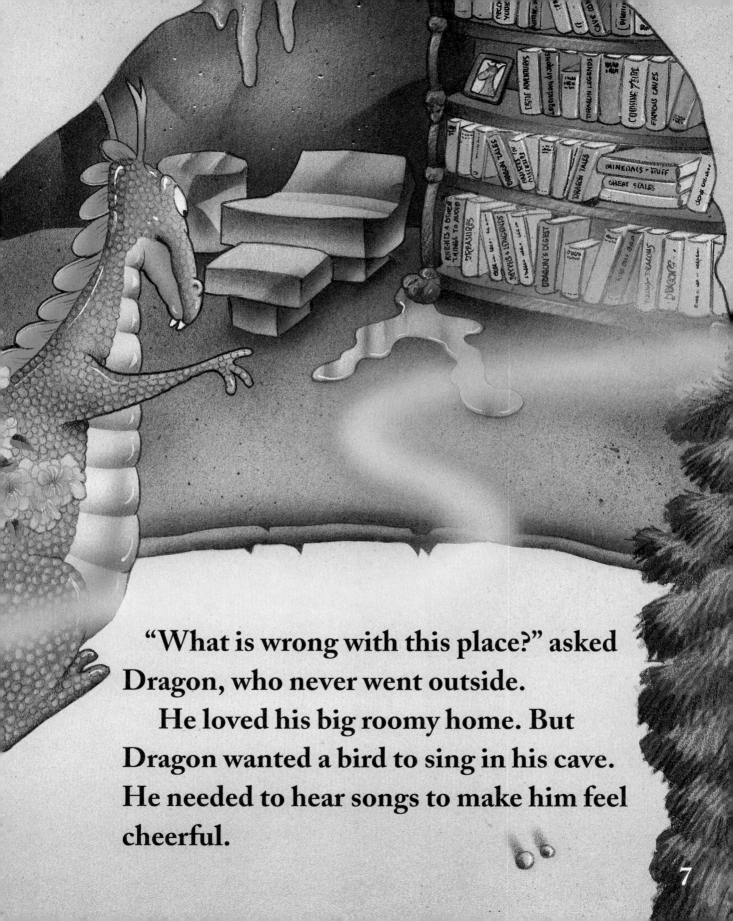

"What is wrong with this place?" asked Dragon, who never went outside.

He loved his big roomy home. But Dragon wanted a bird to sing in his cave. He needed to hear songs to make him feel cheerful.

"Look how dark it is," said Lark.
"I couldn't sing in a dim gloomy cave.
You must light some candles and
make it bright and shiny!"

8

Dragon looked at his cave. The darkness made him feel warm and cozy. He liked to sit in the middle of it and read.

But Dragon wanted a bird to sing in his cave. He needed to hear songs to make him feel cheerful.

"Feel how soggy it is!" said Lark.
"I couldn't sing in a damp wet place. You
must get a towel and wipe it up!"

10

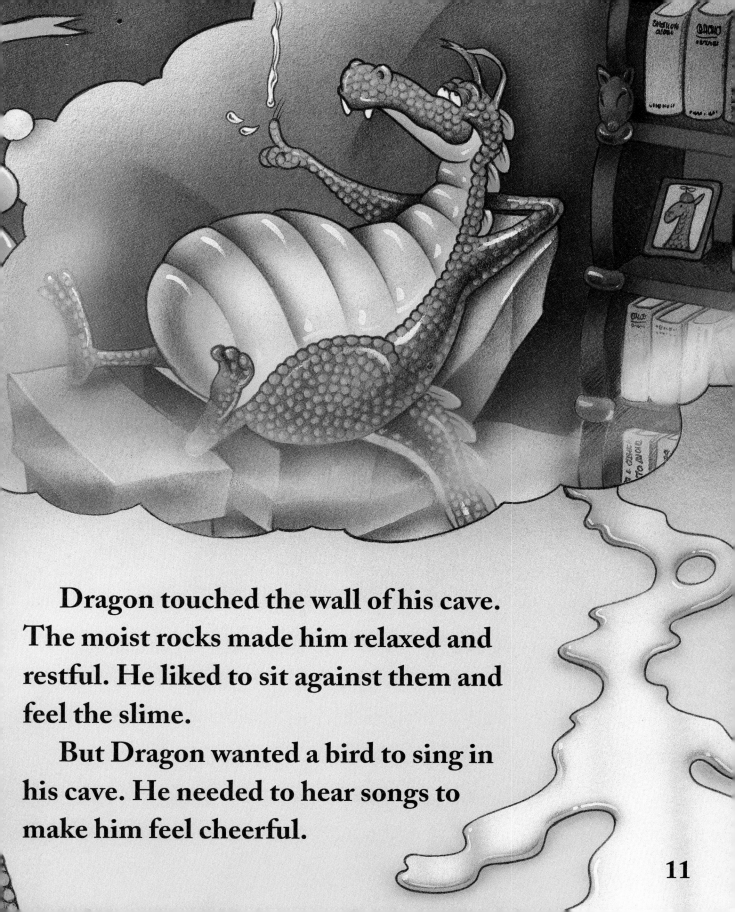

Dragon touched the wall of his cave.
The moist rocks made him relaxed and
restful. He liked to sit against them and
feel the slime.

But Dragon wanted a bird to sing in
his cave. He needed to hear songs to
make him feel cheerful.

"Smell how stale the air is!" said Lark.
"I couldn't sing in this moldy musty
place. You must get a fan and blow in
fresh clean air!"

12

Dragon smelled his cave. The stale air made him feel snug and comfortable.

13

Still, Dragon wanted a friend for his cave. He needed to hear her songs to make him feel cheerful.

Still, Lark needed someone to listen to her songs.

Dragon looked at Lark. Lark looked
at Dragon. All at once, they both knew
what to do.

They could make each other happy!
Each day, Dragon strolls outside his
cave as Lark sings Dragon's song in the
fresh morning air.